This Walker book belongs to:

....

....

For Mom, Cindy and Elieanna, and also for Franny

First published in Great Britain 2010 by Walker Books Ltd
87 Vauxhall Walk, London SE11 5HJ

2 4 6 8 10 9 7 5 3 1

© 2008 Randy Cecil

The right of Randy Cecil to be identified as author/illustrator of this work has been asserted
by him in accordance with the Copyright, Designs and Patents Act 1988

This book has been typeset in Malonia Voigo

Printed in China

British Library Cataloguing in Publication Data:
a catalogue record for this book is available from the British Library

ISBN 978-1-4063-2492-1

www.walker.co.uk

DUCK

Randy Cecil

WALKER BOOKS
AND SUBSIDIARIES
LONDON • BOSTON • SYDNEY • AUCKLAND

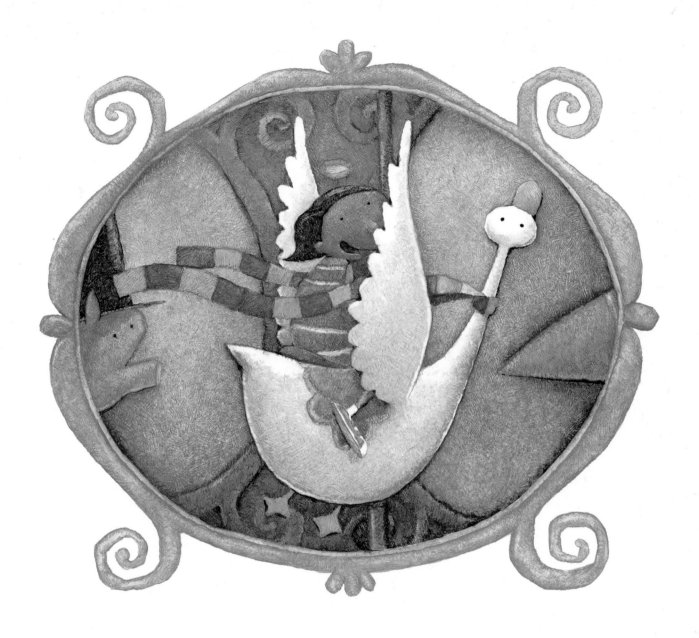

Duck was a merry-go-round animal who longed to fly. She knew her carved wooden wings were not made for flying. But she couldn't stop thinking about it, even when the merry-go-round was whirling.

At night, after the crowds had gone home and the fairground was quiet, Duck would leave her place on the merry-go-round. She loved to watch real ducks soar across the sky.

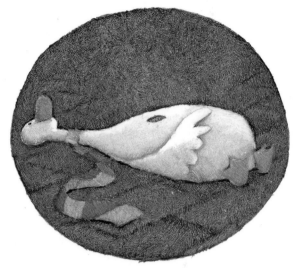

She would lie down on the cobblestones
and look up at the stars. She wondered how
close flying ducks could get to the stars.

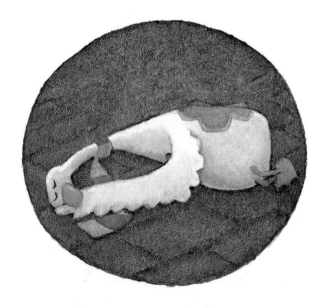

And when Duck fell asleep,
she dreamed she was among them.

Then one spring day,
everything changed. A little lost duckling
ambled through the front gate and
walked right up to Duck.

What's this? wondered Duck.
It had a beak like a duck and feet like a duck.
But she had never seen such a small duck before,
or one so yellow and fuzzy.

She picked up the tiny thing
to examine it more closely.
"Are you a duck?" she asked.
"Quack!" said Duckling.

From that moment on, Duck and Duckling
were always together.

They laughed together.

They played together.

They even dreamed the
same dreams together.

As time passed, Duckling's yellow fuzz turned
into beautiful white feathers and his little wings
began to look like flying ducks' wings.
Soon he was mastering real duck things like
digging through the mud for insects.

But he showed no signs of flying.
If Duckling was ever going to fly, Duck decided
she would have to teach him.

So they began Duckling's training.

In the mornings,
they worked on jumping.
A good jump is
essential for take-off.

Next came flapping
practice. Anyone will
tell you how important
flapping is for flying.

Then Duck would help
Duckling climb up on her
back so Duckling could
feel the wind on his
wings as the merry-go-
round turned.

There were wonderful
moments when
it looked like Duckling
might take off and
fly straight up to
the clouds.

B ut he never quite did.

Duck knew it was time to find the ones who
could teach Duckling what she could not.

So Duck strapped Duckling tightly to her back with
her scarf and set off in search of real ducks.

She walked and walked.
Then suddenly she saw
them – a group of ducks
floating in a stream.

"Now remember
to be polite," she said
to Duckling as she
straightened some of
his new feathers.
"You're going to be fine."

But when she looked for the ducks again,
they were gone.

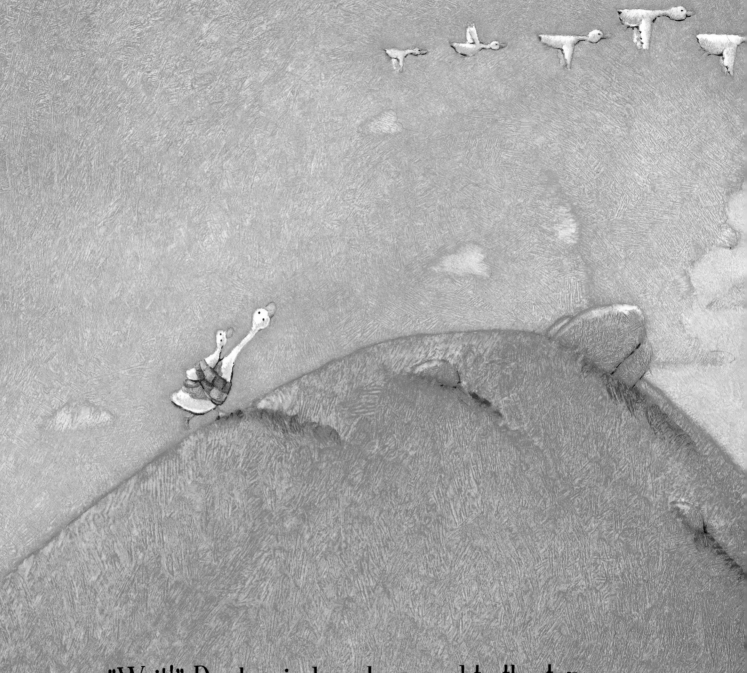

"Wait!" Duck cried as she raced to the top
of a hill. The real flying ducks were high in the sky,
heading south. What if they never found them again?
How would Duckling learn to fly?

Then something magical happened.

They were flying! Sort of.

Duckling was flying, but actually they were
sinking more than they were flying.
Duck was just too heavy for Duckling.

As they sank lower and lower,
Duck realized what she had to do.

She freed herself from the scarf.
Straight away, Duckling went up.

And Duck went down.

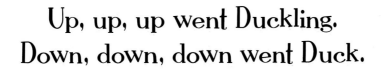

Up, up, up went Duckling.
Down, down, down went Duck.

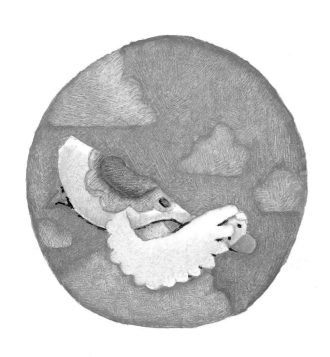

Duck kept going until she hit the ground and skidded to a stop. She looked up just in time to see Duckling taking his place among the other real ducks.

A moment later they were gone.

Duck limped back home to the fairground,
alone and scarfless, to face the long winter ahead.

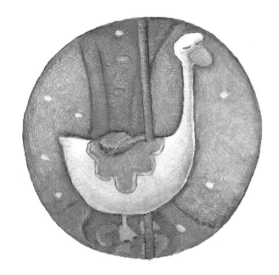

And a long winter it was.

It snowed and snowed.

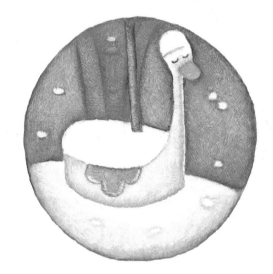

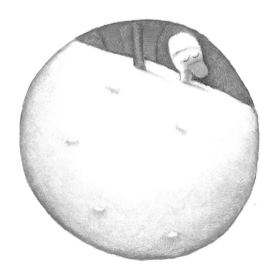

It snowed so much,
Duck almost disappeared.

But finally, spring returned.
The snow melted away, and Duck was
awakened by the bright sun. ,

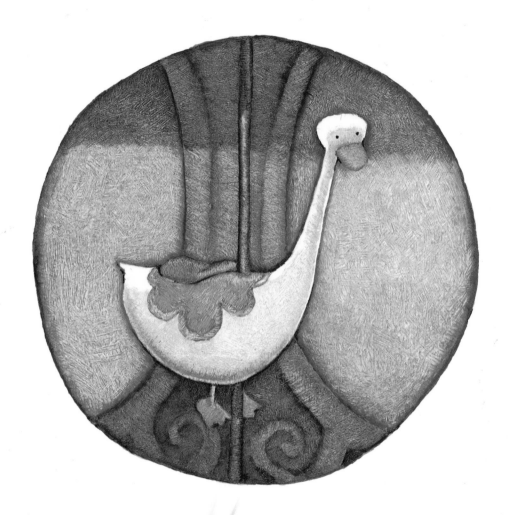

The real ducks were returning, too. But Duck
no longer wanted to watch them fly. It was flying
that had taken Duckling away from her.

Duck sat at the edge of the
merry-go-round and lowered her head.
Then, out of the corner of her eye,
she saw something. . .

It was a real flying duck. But not just any duck. This one was wearing Duck's scarf and flying right towards her. "Duckling!" she cried. "Quack!" said Duckling.

"Let me look at you!" said Duck. "You're all grown up." Duckling preened as Duck patted his head and smoothed his tail feathers.

All that day they laughed together

and played together,

just as they had so many times before.

As night came, Duckling prepared
to leave again with his flock. But first, Duckling
helped Duck climb up on his back.

And finally, Duck knew what it was to fly.